Painted SIDEWALK
MEETING MR. SOSA

TEE RIOS

The contents of this work, including, but not limited to, the accuracy of events, people, and places depicted; opinions expressed; permission to use previously published materials included; and any advice given or actions advocated are solely the responsibility of the author, who assumes all liability for said work and indemnifies the publisher against any claims stemming from publication of the work.

All Rights Reserved
Copyright © 2022 by Tee Rios

No part of this book may be reproduced or transmitted, downloaded, distributed, reverse engineered, or stored in or introduced into any information storage and retrieval system, in any form or by any means, including photocopying and recording, whether electronic or mechanical, now known or hereinafter invented without permission in writing from the publisher.

Dorrance Publishing Co
585 Alpha Drive
Suite 103
Pittsburgh, PA 15238
Visit our website at *www.dorrancebookstore.com*

ISBN: 978-1-6853-7241-5
eISBN: 978-1-6853-7780-9

Painted SIDEWALK
MEETING MR. SOSA

MEETING MR. SOSA: THE BEGINNING

"Can you please hurry up?" Kim asked.

"Kim, baby, why are you rushing? It's not like we going to be late," Tee said.

"It's not about being late. It's about being on time, baby," Kim whined.

Ring, ring, ring....

"Fuck, who's calling this early? Who dis?" Tee spat.

"How come I can't go? Why is she going and not me? Do Kim know we fucking?" the voice asked.

"Bitch, you open yo' mouth, and I'll send you to Cali on three different planes, feel me?" Tee said and meant everything he just said.

"Baby, I just wanted to be with you, that's all," the voice said sleepily.

"Okay, I get it. But, on this trip, Kim and I must go alone. Just remember it was Kim that put all dis together... remember that," Tee said nicely.

"Okay, will I see you when you get back?" she asked.

"Yeah, yeah, no doubt. I got you," I said respectfully.

"Alright, I'll see you when you get back," she said sleepily.

Kim and I arrived at the airport (Columbia). Hell, another long-ass flight. Well, that's what Kim was saying. I said to her, "Chill the fuck out! We're almost there."

"I'm getting sick of being up in the air. I should have stayed home...."

"Wish you would have," I said to myself. "Aren't you tired of being on this thing?"

"No, baby, not tired at all. But (hold on, I'm thinking of something nice to say; oh, yeah)... bitch, shut the fuck up! And stop talking negative! You been crying since we got on this fucking thing, now shut the fuck up. Thank you," said Tee without looking at her. She just looked at me with her head sideways (you know how a dog do it). Finally, as quiet... I gave her a sleeping pill, the bitch was getting on my last nerve. I wanted to kill her in her sleep. Great thought, but I needed her.

Kim and I were about to set it off. Colombian bosses made a deal with both of us, if they learned Kim was dead, deal off and I'm dead. So I kept cool!!!

Five hours later...

"Kim, baby, wake up, we're here," I said as I woke her up.

"Thanks, Papi, how lothro I out?" Kim asked as she looked at Tee; oh, shit, here come a lie.

"About twenty minutes."

"I don't like to lie, but fuck it, the bitch got on my nerves," Tee said and smiled.

"Damn, seems like it was longer than that," Kim said.

"Baby, you just woke up, don't talk right now, please!!!" I said kinda rudely, and again, she turned her head like a dog, putting her hand to her mouth to check to see if her shit stinks (it does). "Baby, when we get to the hotel go to the bathroom and handle that. One more thing, don't talk, please."

Kim said nothing.

We got to the hotel about nine that night. We got showered, brushed our teeth, and went to the club to meet Mr. Sosa, the big boss.

"Damn, the music is pumping, oh, shit, they playing our music," I said to Kim.

"It Takes Two" was playing. Those speakers was banging, damn nere knocked me off my feet.

"Baby, this place is nice," Kim said.

"Yeah, it is," I said, and that's all I said.

"Mr. Sosa will see you now," this big-ass dude said.

"Baby, who dat?"

"I don't know, now please shut the fuck up!!" I said rudely.

Five big-ass men got up from their seats, but the other man that was well dressed remained seated. This must be the one we needed to meet. Mr. Sosa himself.

"Damn, dude is little as hell," I said to myself.

Mr. Sosa just looked us up and down.

"Nice to—"

The tiny man put up his hand and said, "I didn't ask you to speak, but, what I do need is for you two, is to walk with me and say nothing."

Rude mufucka, I should off his ass, thinking to myself.

"I don't like being rude, but walls have ears. Now, please, what was it you was about to say?" Mr. Sosa asked.

I put out my hand, and we began shaking.

"Very nice to meet you, this lovely lady right here is my wife, Kim."

He looked at Kim and smiled. "Nice to meet you both. Please come, I want to show you something."

Kim and I walked with Mr. Sosa. We came to this big-ass building.

"What is this place?" Kim asked.

"Kim, baby, I don't know," I said to her.

Mr. Sosa looked at us without blinking and said, "We are at the beginning of your new life. This is where I make my product, and this is where I sell it." Then he added, "I'm going to give you the very best product money can buy.... These three tables are for you. I know you can handle it...." He paused, cleared his throat, and continued. "50,000 kilos is what you are looking at. No more, no less. Now to be straight up with you," he paused again, then said, "however, if you fuck me over, I will make your family and you very unhappy."

This big fucking dude cocked a super AR15.

"Please understand, this is business."

Kim and I both said, "We understand."

Mr. Sosa looked at us and smiled. "Come, take a look."

He gave Kim and me binoculars (get the fuck outta here). He had a man tied to a bus, and at top speed (bam), against a fucking wall!!!

"Ruthless" was all Tee could think of.

Then a smile came across my face. Just to think, Mr. Sosa was on my side. "I don't know what he has done, hope he learned his lesson." (Well, he won't be in my next book, you know what I'm saying.)

Mr. Sosa looked at me and laughed. After we talked business, Mr. Sosa said, "Do you two dance?"

Kim and I smiled, then we responded, "Yes."

"Come, let's go, enough business, let's have some fun."

"This club is nice. All these fine-ass women," Tee said to me.

Oh, shit, Kim was about to talk.

"Baby, this place is the shit, why we don't have a spot like this in Philly?" Kim asked.

Okay, I was trying to be nice, but this bitch asked too many dumb-ass questions, so here I go.

"How the fuck am I supposed to know why this type of club ain't in Philly? Do it look like I'm a fucking club builder or something, damn.... Kim, I really love you, I do, but I'm 'bout to do some gun-fu on your ass."

Damn, my Chris Tucker was getting better and better, I thought to myself.

"Come join him at his table," the big Colombian said and paused.

Meanwhile, back in Philly...

"Yo, what the fuck. Nigga, you lost your mind? Stealing from the boss, Tee find out, yo ass gonna be a winner of a wet nightmare contest," Marc said.

"Nigga, he ain't gonna find out... 'cause yo ass ain't gone tell him. Besides, he don't give a fuck 'bout you! All I want is what belongs to me anyway."

The new dude said, "Vic, that's yo name, right? You in Tee's room where he lay his head, and you in his safe where he keeps his money. And that's the money he needs to buy more candy. And yo ass in here stealing?"

Marc took his eyes off his buddy.

Click, click.

"Nigga, anybody tell you, you talk too much?"

Now Marc, being the dude he was, knowing not to come empty-handed, pulled out them twins, and with one swift move Marc trained them on Vic's head.

"Nigga, that was a dummy move. Fuck you thinking," Marc said in a whisper, and without one more thought, *kaboom...* right between Vic's eyes, just like that, quickly Marc popped a cap in Vic's head, ending what Vic thought he was about to do.

Back in Columbia...

Tee took a break from being nasty to Kim (well, pay attention).

"Kim, baby, I never told you that you look beautiful. I mean, I've been under lots of stress, and I kinda took that out on you. Baby, I'm sorry. I mean that. Please forgive me. Didn't mean anything by it," Tee said sincerely.

"Baby, I understand. You was being balls and not a dick. And I do forgive you always," Kim said sleepily, and she then added, "Tee, I'm sorry for cheating on you, I don't know what I was thinking, I did something really fucked up and I'm so sorry.... Please, baby, forgive me."

He looked at Kim like she was stupid and didn't say a word.

"Come on, let's dance" was all that was said, for now.

Meanwhile, "Boss, you think this will work? I mean niggers always fuck up. They have no control. They seem to bring attention to them self, then go to jail. I say we dump their bodies in the gator pit. And keep it moving," Mr. Sosa's bodyguard said.

"Tee, he's ruthless, I can see it in him. He will work out. It's his woman I really want.

Hell, if I could have her I will be completely powerful because she is powerful. I am a powerful man, don't get me wrong. But she'll bring more to my table. Understand?" Mr. Sosa said.

After that the bodyguard walked away knowing just what Mr. Sosa meant, Mr. Sosa normally got what he wanted. And right now, he wanted Kim. He had to close his jacket because his dick was getting hard just thinking about Kim.

"Mr. Sosa would like to speak with you," the bodyguard said.

"Hold up, I'm coming," Tee said.

"Not you, just her."

They walked down this dark hall, turned and coming to a closed door, the bodyguard knocked on the door where Mr. Sosa was.

"Come in," Mr. Sosa said.

"You wanted to see me?" Kim asked.

Mr. Sosa looked at Kim with lust in his eyes. Then said, "Let me be straight with you. You are a powerful woman, and I like that in you and you're beautiful. I need someone like you to run my affairs. Run the business, keep things straight. I need you, Kim," Mr. Sosa said boldly. "You would make me a happy man if you were mine," Mr. Sosa said with a devilish smile on his face.

"I thank you for your offer, but I love my husband. And most of all, I'm loyal," Kim said with an attitude.

"I understand," Mr. Sosa said with anger.

Pop, pop, pop. Gunshots rang out.

"What the fuck is going on out there?" Kim asked.

Now one thing about Kim, she was always on point.

She knew something was about to go down. So when Mr. Sosa looked away from her (bad move), Kim pulled her 25 Smith and Wesson and pointed it right at Mr. Sosa. When he turned around, he was looking down the barrel of Kim's heat!

"What the fuck is going on?" Kim asked with fire in her eyes.

After Kim asked that question, *boom,* the door was kicked opened.

"They're all dead, you short mufucka. Set me up. You bitch—"

Before Tee could speak another word, *boom, boom* went Kim's gun.

"Now what?" asked Kim as she looked down at the bleeding body.

"We get the fuck out, we walk out this place, take our shit and bounce. Just like that," Tee responded.

Tee went inside Mr. Sosa's pockets, looking for keys that went to the back door so they could leave. But Kim noticed something: Mr. Sosa wasn't dead.

"What the fuck, this bitch ain't dead!" Kim said.

"Thought you shot him?" Tee questioned.

"I did, this mufucka must have nine lives and shit. I'll kill him this time," she said, pulling out that heat.

"Wait, don't kill him just yet, he's our ticket outta here," said Tee.

Tee grabbed Mr. Sosa off the floor. He had his mini Uzi 9mil. pointed at the half-dead man's head.

"You are my way outta here, now where's the fucking keys? And please don't make me ask again," Tee demanded.

Mr. Sosa was really angry, but hurt, too hurt to do anything.

"Where's the fucking key, you little bitch?" asked Kim with rage in her voice.

"Think you can get away with this? You can't. There's more out there," Mr. Sosa pointed at the door, "and they are going to kill you and your bitch."

Tee hit him so hard he broke Mr. Sosa's jaw (*crack*)....

Tee now whispered, "I'm going to enjoy killing you, but, first things first," Tee said with a smile. "You are going to help put this shit in that truck," Tee pointed. "Then, when we are finished, I might let you go," Tee said, but lied. Tee's thing, no witnesses, no telling, no nothing.... Leaving no tracks, nothing to tie anything to him or Kim!!! (Well, things do happen.)

When they were finished loading the truck with the fifty thousand keys of coke, Mr. Sosa looked at them and said, "What's next, if you're gonna kill me then get it over with. But, remember one thing, if you do, you're dead, if you don't you're dead, so you see, you still lose," Mr. Sosa said with a smile, a very bloody crooked smile.

"How I see it, I win. You lose. Because you're coming with me. And you will tell your men to stand down. So again, I win, you lose, Mr. Sosa," Tee said with a smile, a very well-knowing smile, which meant game over (for Mr. Sosa). Tee put a gun to Mr. Sosa's head, then said, "Point the way out, and if you do anything stupid lights out, you understand?"

Mr. Sosa just looked at Tee without a blink, the man was keeping it gutta. Two of Mr. Sosa's men was standing where Tee and Kim needed to be. They were blocking the gate, but this wouldn't stop nothing. Tee was gangsta on the highest level.

"Don't you dare, you stay cool we all live, one sound, you all die!"

As they were walking to the truck, Mr. Sosa stepped on a twig (*snap*) and one of his bodyguards turned around.

Tat, tat, tat, tat, tat, tat, tat.

Tee and Kim let loose, and it became bullets and gun smoke. They both had AK47s and they was not playing. Kim opened on one dude and shot the man's dick off. Damn, hate to be him, Tee thought.

Tee pulled Mr. Sosa by his arm, running to the truck, that was when Mr. Sosa fell down like a white woman in a scary movie. They managed to get away, as they thought. Two more of Mr. Sosa's men was on their ass, Mr. Sosa got in the truck and started laughing,

"I told you, you will not get away with this, my men will kill you."

Kaboom, kaboom!

"What the fuck was that?" Kim asked.

"That's you two dying, this will be over soon!" said Mr. Sosa.

The men behind them kept shooting.

"Kim, shoot back, bust dat shit down. Give them a taste of Philly!" said Tee.

Kim had no understanding of someone trying to hurt her or her husband, she grabbed the fully loaded AK47 with a double banana clip.

"Shoot, bitch, shoot!"

"What fuck you think I'm doing?" she said as she tried to get off a shot. But Tee was hitting all kinds of potholes in the road, making it hard for Kim to blaze.

"Can't you go any faster? These bitches are gaining, and your ass is driving like Ms. Daisy! Kim!"

"What?"

"Shut the fuck up and shoot!" Tee said.

Kim got mad and let loose, she was fucking them up. Her AK47 was spitting.

"Die, mufuckas, die!!!"

"Keep shooting, we almost there!"

"Tee."

"Yeah?"

"Shut the fuck up and drive, get us the fuck outta here!"

Tat, tat, tat, she was letting loose. Tee hit another ditch and Kim hit the trigger on her weapon. After hitting the bump, Kim was bouncing around in the truck, and a bullet went straight in the window of the car she was shooting at, and hit the driver in the head. What the fuck, that was a good shot, Kim thought to herself.

"That's what you get, you bitch. Did your mother teach you to duck when somebody is shooting at you, game over, bitch."

The car Kim was shooting at went out of control. "Damn, that car is hot," Kim said to herself and laughed, flipping over and over, then the car went up in flames and blew up.

"What happened, what was that?" Mr. Sosa asked.

"That's your men dying," Tee said with a smile.

They made it to the chopper, until the other bodyguards came with fire and gun smoke and started letting their Mack 10s talk. Then more shots was fired, *tat, tat, tat, tat, tat, tat, tat!!*

"Do these fuckers ever die?" Kim asked, then her and Tee let it rain fire, killing the other bodyguard. Kim walked over to the dead man and started shooting the man's already dead body. "Now stay dead, mother fucker. Tee."

"Yeah?"

"Can we leave now? I'm hungry."

They both started laughing. They finally took the keys of coke out the truck and loaded the cocaine on the chopper. Then he looked at the bloody man and forced him on the chopper and then told the pilot to take off.

The man said, "No speakka English."

Kim put that heat to the man's head and said, "Understand now?"

"Si."

He put it in gear and took off. Kim and Tee just busted up laughing. Then realized they had Mr. Sosa.

"What about him?" Kim asked.

"Hand me that rope," said Tee.

"Well, Mr. Sosa, you really came to the end of the line, this is where you get off, have a nice trip."

Tee put the rope around Mr. Sosa and made sure it was tight. Tying the rope to the seat of the choppa, Tee looked at the bloody man. Mr. Sosa was screaming, trying to fight, but lost the battle. Kim pushed the bloody man off and Tee looked at Mr. Sosa, kicked his legs, and then Tee cut the rope and Mr. Sosa was no more. They were up some fifteen thousand feet off the ground. Yeah, that's going to hurt, Kim thought.

Meanwhile, the helicopter arrived at the airport safely. All five thousand keys of coke was placed on the plane safely. The Columbian cartel came to it end, thanks to Tee and Kim. Good move or a bad one, they got what they came for.

"Well, baby, we did it. It's fucked up, the shit we had went through, but we are safe and going home."

"I wonder, did he learn to fly?"

"Who, baby?" Kim asked.

"Mr. Sosa, of course."

Kim and Tee looked at each other and laughed. That was funny too them, for now! They arrived safely in Philly, Tee had some of his men come and help with the shipment. This was no small deal, this was major. Tee had this song stuck in his head ("cash rules everything around me, cream, get the money dollar, dollar bill, y'all"). He loved Wu Tang.

After they loaded up everything, Tee told his men to meet him at the spot. When they arrived at the spot, Tee had a visitor.

"What the fuck are you doing here?? And how the fuck you get in here?"

Fire was coming from Tee's mouth. Every word was thunder and lightning, not holding anything back!

"I just wanted to see you, that's all. Besides, it looks to me you can use my help," the voice responded kindly.

"I don't need your fucking help!"

Boom went the room after Tee raised his voice.

"Now get the fuck outta here, before I let my men chop you down."

Click, click was the sound of Glock 19s around the person Tee was talking to. *Click, clack* was the sound of Gucci shoes hitting the ground as the person was leaving. This was not a joke to Tee, nor a game Tee was playing. He was very serious about his business.

Later that day Tee went home, he needed to talk to Kim. They now had it all. Money, power, and respect, as he thought.

"Kim, are you home, need to talk. Kim, where you at? Are you upstairs sleeping?"

Tee walked all over the house looking for Kim. One more room, the kitchen. *Click, click, click, click* was the sound Tee dreaded to hear.

"Who the fuck are you?" Tee asked, with fire coming from his voice.

"Sit, join your wife."

"Answer my question. Who the fuck are you?"

"My name is Snow, Snow Johnson. Why did you kill him?" Snow asked.

"Don't know what you are talking about. Kill who?"

Bam, bam, slap, slap, this big dude kept hitting Tee.

"Again, why did you kill Mr. Sosa? I supplied him, and you fucked up my money by killing him. So, I want to know, why did you kill him?" Snow asked in a calm voice.

"How am I to know by killing him would fuck up your money? Lady, I don't know you. How did you get in here anyway?" Tee asked.

"I rang the bell, your wife answered, and here I am. The question still remains, why?" asked Snow.

"Sosa tried to fuck me over, he tried to kill me so he can have Kim. So, because I don't like being played, I let loose on him and his men."

"Mr. Sosa have over fifty men watching him, and just the two of you took out Sosa and his men?" Snow paused and then said, "Trent, that is your name, right? Trent? I'm not going to kill you two so calm down, but now you work for me! And this is not negotiable, you two belong to me!" Snow said as she stood up.

"Since you're standing, get the fuck out, and to let you know, we don't belong to no one!" said Tee as he pointed at him and Kim.

"Ha, ha, ha, ha, that's what you think!" Snow said with authority, and just like that they got ghost her and her men.

"Whatever" was all Tee said.

Kim and Tee just met the big boss, the real boss, Snow Johnson, the head of the Triads, a true gangsta.

"Kim, get the guys together, we just ran into a big problem," he ordered.

Tee was not Snow, because Snow ran the biggest drug chain everywhere. But, Tee was far from dumb. And he knew how to move. And he knew what candle he just lit.

A moment later the phone rang.

"Kim, answer the phone."

When Kim answered she recognized who it was.

"Baby, that fool Marc is on the phone. He said something about the time of a meeting? I told him that you can't come to the phone. But he said he needed to speak to you," said Kim as she handed over the phone.

"What's good, fam? How's everything?" Tee asked.

"Yo, fam, I had to off that nigga Vic!" said Marc, still a little angry due to killing Vic.

"Why did you kill him? He was a good worker. At least, that's what you told me!"

"Wait, what you saying, nigga? The nigga Vic was trying to steal from you in your house! That's why I put two to his dome."

"Hold on, Vic the new dude was trying to get me for my paper, in my house." He pointed at his self like it was hard to understand. "That's why money been short, he's been doing this shit for minute. Fuck-ass nigga. I should kill his family for that shit! Feel me?"

Tee was fuming but maintained to be calm, he spoke in a low-tone voice. Stealing was bad when everyone was eating. But to steal from Tee, that would cause the sidewalk to be painted!

"Fam, is it clean?"

"Yeah, it's straight."

"Good, round up everyone and meet me at the spot."

"What time?"

"You know the time."

Click and dial tone.

Everyone came to the meeting. They all was dressed like they stepped out of an urban GQ magazine. Big gold chains, diamond rings and fur coats, and everyone was pushing a nice-ass car. Lamborghini, Bentley, Jaguars, just to name a few. They was living the life, like all people that had millions.

"Thank you all for coming, we have in our hands the best product money can buy, but tonight I need to tell you about a problem, I give this warning. Be on your p's and q's, there is a roaring loin loose, and her name is Snow Johnson. She is the head of the Triads in San Fran, that's California for all you dumb mafuckkas." Tee smiled while saying that. "Don't get caught slipping!! And do not let her beautiful looks and her fine-ass body fool you. Real talk, my niggas. This woman is fine, and very dangerous." Tee paused, then continued. "Make sure you stay strapped, keep your shit ready to bust no matter what, because she's ready to kill no matter what." Now looking around the room, looking for weakness in his men. "There should always be two or more on the block. One, and you are a dead mother fucker!! Threes, gentlemen, stay in threes. This woman will set you on fire, then ask you questions. Now, do you have any questions?" Tee thought of something he almost forgot. "I almost forgot, the next time one of you think of going into my fuckin' house and jacking me, bitch, think twice. Now get the fuck out!"

All his henchmen and his street boys got up and walked out the door. Meeting over!

Meanwhile, at Tee's house: *knock knock knock.*

"Who the fuck knocking on my door like that?" Kim opened the door and Kim's eyes got big. She thought she was seeing a ghost! "Bitch, I killed you. How the fuck?"

"Hello, baby, missed me? Always shoot your enemies in the head. Isn't that what you told me? So they can never come back. Remember that? Well, I'm back, bitch! Now, where do you want it? The head or the head? Oops, same choice. Let me see, you rather have me get over and done with. So I choose the head!"

"Baby, I'm home," Tee said as he interrupted what he thought was a regular conversation between Kim and somebody. Then he looked up. "What the fuck are you doing in my house? Give me that."

Tee was trying to take a loaded gun from the person that was holding it. *Clack, clack:* the gun went off and Tee fell to the floor. Blood was coming out fast. And he was fading fast. It was getting dark, quiet, no movement, no nothing.

The end had come quickly.

Wait one minute, wtf. No no no, hold up, this is not going to end like this!!! Talking about the end. The end my ass. Finish this shit!

"Hey, there's my man. Are you okay, baby? I thought I lost you."

Tee couldn't speak a word. He had all kinds of tubes in his mouth. A moment after Kim asked her husband was he okay, the hospital door opened.

"What the fuck do you want?" Kim asked in a whisper, not trying to upset her husband by getting loud.

"You can be just a little bit nicer. We are in a hospital, you know."

Kim couldn't hold her anger anymore, she let loose. "I don't care where we at, you need to rise up out of here, before I put my foot in your ass and give you a Rodney King beatdown," said Kim.

"Ooh, baby, that's the pleasure I love. Getting beat and shit. Where's the best place, the bathroom, the floor, or right here on your husband's bed, here in the hospital?"

"Bitch, I fucked you up once before, and I won't mind doing it again! So again, what the fuck do you want?" Kim's anger was coming quickly.

"Everything. Everything you took from me. Bitch, we had everything together, most important, we had each other! And you let someone come between us. Why, Kim, huh, why? All this drama all over some dick. I remember when you didn't like men, said they were nasty, and now, you fuckin' one, oops, my bad, you're married to one. So, when I made it through my surgery and got myself together and got right, I decided to have what you have!"

"And what is that?" Kim asked, rolling her eyes.

"A dick, your man's big, black, juicy dick. And bitch, you're right, his dick is nice and big," looking under the sheets, looking at Kim's husband's dick, "and I will get it...again, and again and again. Well, you know, when he's feeling better."

"Oh, shit" was what Tee thought as the room was spinning. "What the fuck!" Tee got up from the bed, sweating badly, very confused.

Kim ran to see what was going on! "Tee, baby, what's wrong?" Kim asked as she wiped the sweat from Tee's face.

"A dream, or maybe a nightmare. Someone was trying to kill you, I jumped in the middle." Tee was telling Kim what the dream was about. "And, and—"

"And what, baby?"

"I got shot and I thought I was dead. That shit was crazy, babe. I mean it seemed so real."

Kim just looked at her husband like he was crazy. "Baby, why don't you lay back down, I'll go get you something to eat!" Kim said out of concern for her husband.

"That's real nice, Kim, but after that shit, I'm not staying in bed, period. Baby, I have to get up anyway, got things to check on. Imma take a shower, get dressed, then go."

Kim looked confused, she didn't know what to think. Tee knew what he had to do, no dream, no nightmare or anything or anyone can stop him from handling his business, he is on a mission. He had to go see someone, and that someone was Liz, the woman Kim thought she ended. These dreams was all behind her.... If he didn't go see Liz and handle his business, then the dreams and nightmares just wouldn't stop, nor would Liz. So he needed to see Liz, asap.

After he got dressed and did a lookover, he smiled at how good he looked, then he bounced. He didn't waste no time, he didn't say goodbye to his baby Kim.

Tee got in his 130,000-dollar BMW and burnt rubber. He talked to a couple dudes on his way, made sure they was good. Then went to see Liz. 123 West Main Street. The slums of West Philly. Bingo, that's the address, he thought to himself. Tee got out of his car and checked to make sure he had his heat, then he took a deep breath and knocked on the door, it opened. Liz stood there, she was looking so good, Tee's dick got hard fast.

"Liz is looking good, real good," he said in a quiet tone.

"You just going to stand there or are you coming in?" Liz questioned as she was digging the way Tee was looking.

"This nigga looks good as hell. I should suck his dick right here," speaking low to herself. "You know damn well Tee won't go for that shit," talking to herself again.

"We need to talk!" said Tee as he walked in Liz' home.

"Okay, let's talk." Liz' pussy was getting wet looking at him, hoping they would fuck. She started grabbing Tee's dick.

"Bitch, get off me, I didn't come here to fuck, I need to talk to you!"

"Oh, my bad. So what's up?" Liz wanna know.

"Can't see you no more. Shit getting crazy. I'm having bad dreams and shit. Dreaming people tryna kill me, seeing you in my fuckin' dreams and shit. Shit is really crazy, you ask me." Tee spoke boldly.

"So, let me get this shit straight. You come over here every fuckin' night scene you been back home from Columbia, fuckin' me, getting your dick sucked, putting your dick all up in me, fucking me in my ass, shooting cum deep down in my throat, swallowing your shit and now, fucking now, you saying we done. Over some fucking dream! Is that what I just heard? Finished, over a fucking dream. Nigga, are you crazy, leaving me just like that, just completely over? What happened to 'I got your back'? What about that promise, huh, you gas me up with your cum, and just like that," she snapped her fingers, "we done!" She raised her voice. Liz was getting mad.

"Kim, I mean Liz—"

She cut him off before he could say another word. "Now you calling me that bitch's name, really. Bad move on your part, nigga. You got the wrong bitch, and you got the game fucked up, nigga!" yelling with anger.

Liz had no understanding whatsoever for the shit Tee was saying; Liz walked away mad as hell. She then ran to the bedroom, reaching under her pillow, grabbing that heat, the same gun Tee gave her. (Bad move. Never give a crazy woman a gun.) Liz had a little crazy side about her, and she was a gangsta. That was the evil side of her.

Tee walked behind Liz, trying to stay on her heels. When Tee opened the door that Liz slammed, *boom, boom, boom.* He moved out the way, reaching for his pistol, he shot back and kept shooting until there was no movement. A scream rang out. It was Liz in pain, Tee shot her 17 times. She became a winner of a wet t-shirt contest, Liz was bloody. Leaking badly.

She looked up at Tee. "I really did love you, now I'm going to die for the love I have in me. I love you, baby," Liz said.

She took a deep breath, then pointed to her stomach, trying to tell Tee something, then she died. She never got a chance to tell Tee she was pregnant with his baby. Tee had no feeling about this. Until he realized what she was pointing at. It was too late. He killed Liz and his baby. Liz was carrying a baby for him. That was what he came to do anyway. Right. To kill Liz. He didn't knowing she was having his baby, he came to kill Liz, not a baby. To take Liz out the game. Killing Liz was on his mind, not kill a baby. That was why he was there in the first place. But, the crazy part of this was he didn't care. The only thing he thought of was to get rid of Liz. (Now at least that shit Liz always said, "One day I'll get you," would never happen.) And to make really sure she would never make that happen, he shot her 4 more times in the head, even though he realized Liz was pregnant with his baby, it was too late anyway so he didn't care (the bitch was dead, fuck it), Tee thought to his self and walking out the door.

Meanwhile, Kim called a meeting with their mafia family. Her husband just walked in. Tee called out for Kim. Then he remembered his crew was there. He didn't realize he had so many workers. Men and women sat at his table. The men was straight-up killers but women was worse than the men. They wouldn't give a second thought about killing a person, they did everything Tee asked of them.

"Shh, listen up. Kim have something to say," Marc announced, quieting the room.

"Tee and I want you to be on point. Snow Johnson is the head of the Triads, now how that happened I don't know. But, word on the street says she'll put a hit on anyone of this family that don't cooperate. She also says that we are breakfast, lunch, and dinner to her. She want us to work for her, which will never happen. And if we won't work for her, then she will kill us! As she think. And that's not going to happen either. Tee and I sent a message. And the message was, sending her an ear that used to belong to one of her henchmen. And we gave her another message by means of another so-called killer that was caught slipping, he also was caught slipping, we told her to go fuck herself." Kim paused. "The reason I say it won't happen, simple, she have a weakness. That weakness is her Chinese sister, Rae. Rae's not gangster like Snow." Pause again, making sure everyone was paying attention, they were!

"So, if it came down to it, we snatch baby sister Rae. We will flood the streets of Philly, anyone buying powder, buying from us. Anyone buying crack buying from us, and if Snow's men giving us problems we snatch baby sis. So, stay on your game, watch each other's back, and if you have to bust a cap then bust. Any questions? Good, silence means you got it. Tonight you will get your supplies. I'm sending it to you so get where you need to be, Marc will drop it off to you. This meeting is over!"

Marc was called back by Kim.

"Do you know why I called you back?"

"No, what's up?"

"Next time you bring someone in this family, make sure they are not the police. Do you understand?"

Marc just looked at Kim, confused. "Fuck you talking about? I never brought the police in our family! So, why are you talking like this?" He was getting angry, thinking Kim was picking another argument.

But she wasn't. In fact, Vic, the guy Marc killed, was a cop. Marc didn't do his homework on the guy. The family didn't eat pork.

"That guy Vic, remember him, he was a cop, if you did your homework you would have known. So again, don't bring another cop in here!"

Kim then told Marc to come closer. He did, and Kim kissed him on his cheek and whispered in his ear, "Fuck up like that again and I'll kill you myself. Got me?" Kim was deadly quiet when she spoke to Marc. In a fainted voice Kim said this, and meant every word.

Marc didn't try to argue, he knew Kim was right. Plus he knew he couldn't go against the grain. So Kim was right, he didn't do his homework on Vic and that could have caused a lot of problems for the family.

"Now get the fuck out. Dumb-ass nigga."

Meanwhile in California...

"You going somewhere?" Rae asked Snow.

"Why, you thinking about going with me if I do, little sister?" questioned Snow.

"I'm saying, you should, oh, never mind, just be careful if you do," Rae said, sounding sad.

"Don't worry about me, baby girl. I'll be okay. So tell me. What's go on in Philly?" asked Snow.

"Besides Tee killing two of your men, they're getting bigger and stronger. They had last month two hundred workers, now there are two thousand workers. Looking like a small army if you ask me."

"I didn't ask you, maybe I should go back to Philly to see whose army is bigger," Snow stated, walking back and forth.

Snow had a big responsibility, Rae's father, the boss and head of the Triads, just gave authority to Snow. That was a lot of power and weight on her shoulders. The truth was Snow was scared. Scared that she would fuck up. Scared she couldn't handle that type of leadership. A gangster female, yes. Not a leader!

"Why would you go back to Philly, that would be a suicide mission. And besides the fact that he's fine as hell, and he's smart. And a killer. You should remember, he is the one who took out Mr. Sosa and all of his men. He don't play games, dear sister of mine. Plus he have everyone in his pocket, Snow. You might want to reconsider your thoughts. That was a very powerful statement he made, for just one person. What do you think, sister dearest?" Rae said with a smile, knowing Snow was getting mad for the shit she just said. And in Rae's mind for real, Snow couldn't take on Tee. He did this type of shit for a living. He played "tag, you're it" with your life. Tee once cut a man's eyes out and asked him, "You see what you just made me do?" holding the man's eyes up to him.

"Sounds like you need to choose a side. That's what I think. Sounds like, you don't think I could win against that mother fucker. That's what it sound like to me. So fuck you and fuck Tee. I can win against him and anyone else that go against me. I'm that bitch! I'm the head of this big-ass family, now you remember that. Also, what you need to remember. Your father put me, not you, in charge. Now you remember that shit, lil' sister!"

"All this money, and you still trying to write checks your ass can't cash, now you, miss so fucking powerful queen bitch, you remember that!" Rae said and disappeared.

Snow was so angry at what Rae just said, she pulled out her gun and started shooting everything.

Rae walked down the hall laughing because she knew she just pissed off her so-called sister.

Now back in the room Snow was thinking, "Is it true? Is Tee more powerful than I am? Or can I, the queen of the most dangerous gang, take out Tee and his men? What the fuck did I just get into?"

To be continued...

CPSIA information can be obtained
at www.ICGtesting.com
Printed in the USA
BVHW091915120822
644460BV00014B/1494